Brian
the Smelly Bear
and the Very Smelly Babies

Mark Chambers

BONNEY
PRESS

Published by Bonney Press,
an imprint of Hinkler Books Pty Ltd
45–55 Fairchild Street
Heatherton Victoria 3202 Australia
www.hinkler.com

BONNEY
PRESS

© Hinkler Books Pty Ltd 2017, 2018

Author and illustrator: Mark Chambers
Editorial: Emily Murray

ISBN: 978 1 4889 0025 9

Printed and bound in China

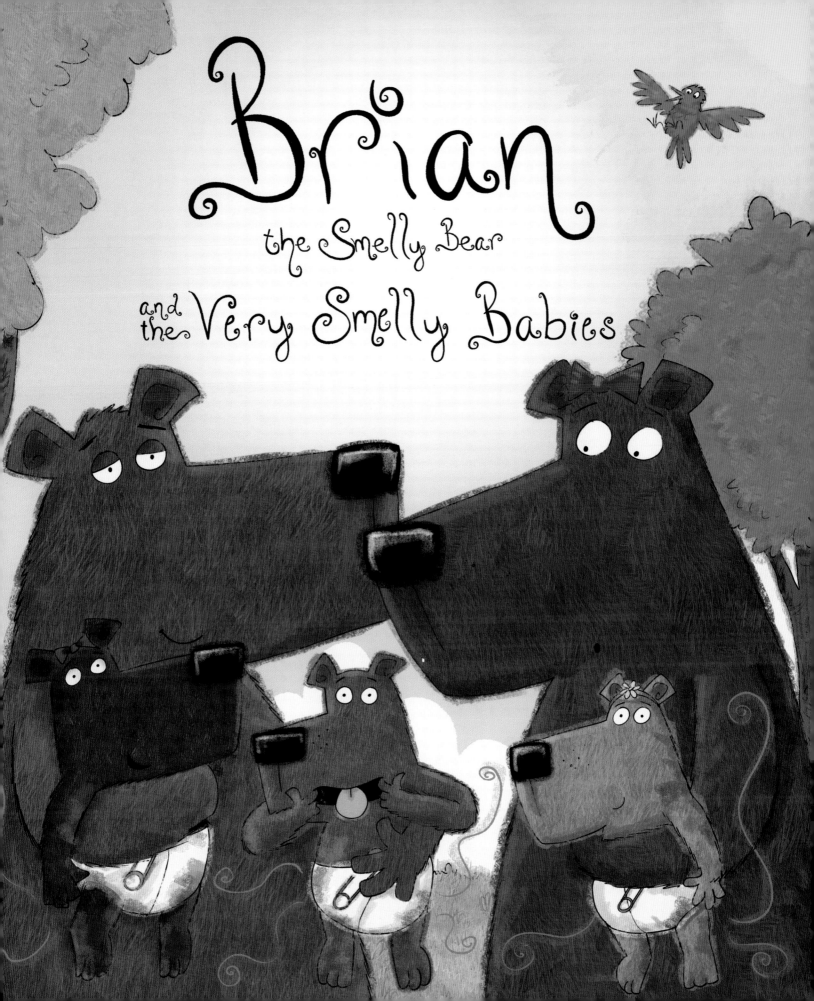

Brian

the Smelly Bear

and the Very Smelly Babies

Brian and Bryony were two happy bears,
living life to the full, without any cares.
They skipped through the woods and slept under the trees,
and they danced around with the birds and the bees.

One sunny morning, Brian opened his eyes,
he'd been woken up by the sound of soft cries.
There before him were three baby bears,
he said to Bryony, "Don't bears come in pairs?"

Now Brian and Bryony had three bundles of joy —
what a lovely family: two girls and a boy.

They fed them

and washed them

and put them to bed,
with a story each night
and a kiss on the head.

Their neighbours popped over and as a surprise,
placed gifts and three cakes in front of their eyes.

Frog gave them a rattle made of wood and some seeds,

and Rabbit gave a blanket he'd knitted from weeds.

The sweet little cubs were passed round one by one,
looking so cute, and having such fun.
Then all of a sudden came an almighty sound,
the sound was so loud that it rattled the ground!

Frog gasped for air and Rabbit hopped off,
Badger felt sick at the horrible BOFF!

Tortoise gulped twice and went back in his shell.
How could something so small make that terrible smell!?

Brian held his nose tight and Bryony went pink,
how could such lovely babies make such a big stink?

"We must wash them at once!" Brian said with a frown.
"These bears are surely the smelliest around!"

So out Brian went and found a big metal tub,
and a big fluffy brush to give the babies a scrub.
After what seemed like hours, those bear cubs were clean,
and gave off a smell that would not turn you green.

Brian and Bryony both sniffed at the breeze,
it no longer ponged of rotten old cheese.

The babies, however, went off in a grump

until one of them let
forth an almighty
"TRUMP!"

Brian thought that the clean-up was finally done,
but the three slipped away to have some more fun.
They found a big swamp, all green, brown and boggy...
in jumped the cubs, getting smelly and soggy!

Brian and Bryony both brought a towel,
"GET OUT OF THAT MUCK!"
they said with a growl.

The little cubs giggled and fell about on the floor.
This time the smell was much worse than before!

By now their friends' noses had caught that strong whiff,
They all cried together, "What a horrible niff!"

Badger said sternly, "Enough is enough!
It's time to clean up these stinkballs of fluff!"

So, Brian and Bryony tried something new,

A SUPER-STRONG NO-PONG FOAM-TASTIC shampoo!

The babies all splashed and made lots of bubbles, and laughed with delight. Would this fix their troubles?

Brian and Bryony had three little bears,
a beautiful family, without any cares.

Because those little cubs, after all that was said...

...thought bath time with bubbles was more fun instead!